I0524253

THE CRYPT OF BLOOD

A HALLOWEEN TV SPECIAL

Jonathan Raab

Illustrations by Mat Fitzsimmons

MUZZLELAND PRESS
Golden, Colorado

ISBN: 978-0-9970803-8-4

Illustrations by Mat Fitzsimmons

Edited by Sean M. Thompson

Cover art by Trevor Henderson

Layout and design by Jonathan Raab

Ravenscroft typeface © Justin Callaghan. Used under commercial license.

Double Feature typeface © David Shetterly. Used under the SIL Open Font License.

Psycho-spiritual disruptions courtesy our national death cult

Published by Muzzleland Press
Golden, Colorado
USA

www.muzzlelandpress.com
www.twitter.com/muzzlelandpress
www.facebook.com/muzzlelandpress

Get the official soundtrack from Black Mountain Transmitter at lysergicearwax.bandcamp.com

For Daniel Myrick, Eduardo Sánchez, and
Stephen Volk

OVERTURE TO A SYMPHONY OF TERROR

Upon a small soundstage nestled deep within the haunted heart of the Front Range Public Access Television Station, three coffins lie in peaceful repose.

Candles flicker and drip wax, plastic skulls leer from the shadows, and heavy fog crawls along the floor of the studio. The image is tinged with static and atmospheric interference. The video cameras recording the proceedings are old—hand-me-downs from the local corporate media affiliate, donated as tax write-offs. The original recording of this broadcast has been transferred or copied across multiple media, again and again, giving the image you see now a grainy and fuzzy look.

A slight static hum underpins the audio track, just as the somber, Gothic church organ-synthesizer score begins, bringing to mind creaky old vampire movies broadcast on Saturday afternoons during your childhood—or the idealized childhood perhaps you wish you had.

The music is meant to be ominous, or, at the very least, spooky—but you find it somehow familiar and comforting. The composition brings to mind memories of microwave popcorn and ice-cold pop on hot summer nights; of fake, orange-red Technicolor blood dripping from false wounds; of staying up too late to watch creature-features with friends or your cousins; of glamorous women in long, flowing dresses creeping through haunted castle corridors; of handsome vampire killers wielding crucifixes and holy water; of wolfmen and mutant creatures born of man's scientific hubris or occult ambitions; of bloodsuckers and mummies emerging from their ancient tombs to stalk the living.

"There comes a season... a season of *darkness*," a local actor says in his best Vincent Price imitation. "A season of madness. When minds are weak to the influences of satanic evil. When the enemies of mankind haunt the fallow fields and darkened byways of our vulnerable domain. When darkness, shadow, and evil itself sits on the throne of power, and the world is ruled by wickedness that wears a mask of righteousness."

The lid on one of the coffins begins to move—slowly, surely. The other lids are moving now, too, as ghoulish, flesh-dripping hands reach up from within.

"There comes a season..."

One of the coffin lids slides off and strikes the stage floor, accompanied by a sound effect like stone striking stone, although the materials are far too flimsy to be anything other than spray-painted balsa wood. But the effect is accomplished through impression, if not form, and the reverb-laden Foley effect lingers on the audio track.

The lids on the other coffins are likewise shoved aside. Their occupants begin to rise, backs straight and arms crossed over their chests, actors in pale grey makeup over a dull green base. Long, crooked fingernails and pointed ear applications. Frilly shirts and ill-fitting dark slacks for the two men on the right; a thick, faded-red dress for the woman on the left, clothes mottled and falling apart, as if robbed from real graves, not pulled from a community theater wardrobe.

"...when the undead thirst..."

The ghouls' eyes snap open, bloodshot and full of a terrible, inhuman hunger.

"...for the blood of the living!"

Those eyes fill the screen in freeze-frame—one set sliding

in along the bottom third, the next in the middle entering from the opposite side, and the eyes of the vampiress gliding in to the top of the stack. The narrator's hearty, villainous laughter cascades and echoes off of old stone walls.

The synthesizer score melts and morphs into an orchestral track pulled from the depths of the TV station's public domain horror movie catalog, crackling with degradation. It swells into a frenzy of pounding drums and high-pitched strings, while a theremin threads its otherworldly notes.

The film title flies forward, hand-painted and dripping like blood:

FRONT RANGE COMMUNITY THEATER PRESENTS:
THE CRYPT OF BLOOD
A HALLOWEEN TV SPECIAL
COPYRIGHT FRCT 2007

Then, fading in from a rolling, animated bank of fog beneath:

INSPIRED BY THE NOVEL THE CRYPT OF BLOOD
BY COUNTESS BLAIR OSCAR WILFLAME

Credits rendered in that blood-dripping typeface cycle through the cast, the stagehands, the director, the producers, and the local sponsors; the Front Range Public Access Television Station camera operators, editor, and sound and visual effects team. With each change of card comes a change in shot, offering a different angle of the stage: slow-moving tracking shots dragging across the tableau of horror, or delightful close-ups of the skulls, candleholders, occult tomes, coffins, costumery, cobwebs, rubber bats on barely visible fishing line, and rolling, spectral-blue underlit fog.

The last of the credits warp and twist into the image of a grinning cartoon skull, which opens its jaw and lurches toward the screen to consume the viewer, passing beyond its limits to leave the image of a single flickering flame in its wake.

That flame is the burning tip of a red candle dripping blood-red wax, set behind an eldritch tome with a black cover and binding, scuffed bronze clasps holding it shut. This grimoire does not look like a cheap prop at all, and on its cover is an emblem of a withered, ruined hand pointing toward heaven and the title:

The Crypt of Blood.

SCENE ONE: BLOODY FOREST

Uneven rows of half-timbered German-style houses stand over old stone roads. Streaks of damage and missing frames imply this footage is pulled from the archives, until the various shots of the burg dissolve to reveal a drone-captured, overhead shot of an unpaved road, presumably leading away from the town.

This road winds away into the wilderness, mountains looming in the background, shrouded in mist. We arrive at a junction within the dark forest where tree branches have lost their leaves, drained of color against the broken grey sky. They assume the countenance of skeletal hands, waving in the chill-bitten wind.

"Ah, what lovely weather for my evening constitutional."

At ground-level now, a shot of a small shrine, dedicated to St. Mary herself, complete with a statue of the Blessed Virgin set within a wooden box with a sloping roof. From the edge of the frame—from existence itself—emerges a gentleman in a fine black overcoat and top hat. He is lanky and tall, and carries a marble-black cane topped by a glass bulb, within which rests flecks of gold reminiscent of those showered upon charismatics in mammon-worshipping houses of sin.

"A day's worth of work for a nobleman such as myself includes moving capital and influence around a chessboard of power and keeping it out of the hands of the lecherous state and the lustful lesser peoples of this doggerel nation," he says, to no one in particular. His delivery is somewhat stilted, although the lines themselves certainly provide no help in that regard.

"I wield my unearned power in a thousand obtuse and petty ways! An evening's walk always clears my mind of such matters, and increases my vigor in preparation for the night's innumerable pleasures."

Fog slithers along the path ahead in tributaries of obscuring grey, linking the undergrowth across both sides of the narrow path. The gentleman pauses briefly to pull tight his coat and cape, and to peer over his shoulder with unease. Something in the distance howls, and its lonely cry echoes and reverberates across the wood and the audio track alike, a reminder that all men are vulnerable in nature's domain.

That howl sound effect is surprisingly *spooky*—a tingling, exciting sensation that crawls along your spine like the fingertips of a ghost. But there's another feeling welling up within you besides the cheap excitement of a low-budget horror movie. A feeling that has been festering in the pit of your stomach since pressing *PLAY* on the VCR—or even earlier.

It really started when you set eyes on the faded and cracked casing of the VHS cassette with *"CRYPT OF BLOOD HALLOWEEN SPECIAL"* hand-scrawled on its peeling label. That feeling has accompanied you every waking moment since, bubbling just beneath the surface of your conscious thoughts, like a troublesome old acquaintance or vice you hoped to leave behind, but never could.

You struggle to hold on to the memory of having the cassette first pressed into your hands. You consider the incomplete and fog-shrouded chain of events that led you to that moment: when you first heard of *The Crypt of Blood* TV movie and what prompted you to seek it out in the first place; what lengths you went to find it; who it was that finally delivered it to you... and at what cost.

There's a sense you *know* these things, but they are shadows of memory, dancing behind your twitching eyeballs like light flickering on a drive-in screen, routed on a network of neural pathways home to the energy flow and misunderstood higher-dimensional processes that are closer to what actually constitutes *mind* than the collection of grey matter tissues and violent neurochemicals you vaguely comprehend as a *functioning brain.*

The more you try to focus on those elusive memories, the further they slip, offering you glimpses of their volume and import.

Burning gasoline in the air of the dank sub-basement of an industrial warehouse. A droning horror-synth soundtrack reverberating up through the ground beneath your feet and up into your roiling insides. Robed figures with pale hands and paler faces beckoning you to venture further into that labyrinth of concrete and particle-board stage walls painted to look like grey stone, such thin veils between the fantastical and the mundane. Pale blue light shines above, beneath, and between the cracks, the only source of illumination in those mind-wearying halls.

You recall turning a corner and coming upon an open space where row after row of tables held scattered horrors or facsimiles thereof: outdated surgical equipment, mannequins and dummies in various states of decay and dismemberment, monster masks and claws and the splayed open biomechanical innards of animatronic horrors.

Lording over it all, the director, the *auteur*, offering you the tape. Who or what he was/is you can't be sure, and you have no desire to know, because to know would be to correlate the contents of your imperfect knowledge. To *know* would be madness.

Currents of foul breath flowing from within the folds of its dark hood. Nostrils flaring on an animal's snout. Eyes within the dark, alight and on yours, seeing you. Seeing *through* you, to the end of you—of what you will become because of what you are tasked with doing. The great work of your otherwise inconsequential life.

His hands are not human, never could have been. Cloven and fur-matted, with large black nails on grotesque, unnatural toe-fingers.

Receiving the tape from those hands like communion. Accepting the key to an analog world of the past, of terror.

Mercifully, your mind releases its hold on that flickering memory, the projector shuttering to a stop.

On your TV screen, the gentleman continues his evening stroll, passing through a narrow neck of the path and poked by barren branches on either side. That unnerving howl goes up again, closer this time, but drawn-out and unnaturally low in pitch, as if it is not from a wolf or dog after all, but something merely affecting the sound of a howl and, this close to the object of its pursuit, it begins to let slip the mask of its deception.

The gentleman pauses to look back. Seeing nothing but fog and the encroaching dark, he turns to continue on his way.

A figure in a flowing, purple-hooded robe with crimson and gold trim stands before the gentleman now, blocking the path forward. As he notices them for the first time, he flinches and his face contorts into a mixture of sudden fright, soon giving way to annoyance.

"Greetings," he says, pushing up the brim of his hat with his cane.

There is no reply. This annoys the gentleman, as he is, like many of his station, not used to being ignored by his *lessers*. The figure stands with its back to him, hood drawn, compounding his frustration. His tone grows curt, in a manner that would typically send those unlucky enough to be in his service into a groveling frenzy of apology.

"Good *evening*," he says. "I am about my constitutional and wish not to be disturbed. You see, I am not accustomed to being bothered in these woods, which has been in my family's possession for—"

Another howl interrupts him. Closer. This sound even less like the cry of a common animal, and even more like something else entirely.

"Very *well*," the gentleman declares, desiring to be gone from this place, and to return to somewhere warm, safe, and sane. "My advice to you is: depart from this wood and path, and leave it to your betters! My servants usually patrol these routes, and do not take kindly to trespassers."

The last sentence comes out of his mouth with difficulty, as he is beginning to realize his men will not be coming down the path—not when he needs them to, now that he is alone and afraid with this odd stranger and the approach of some creature whose imminent appearance causes his very soul to recoil within the confines of its fleshly vessel.

"Good *night* to you, then," he says, tipping his hat and taking a step forward. But as he looks up from his salute, the figure is gone. The path is clear.

He continues his walk at a hurried pace, turning back and forth, eyes searching the narrow path ahead and behind. Nearby vegetation and dead trees are too thick and close for the figure to have cut through. The gentlemen's paranoia is communicated through extreme close-ups of parts of his face—his wide eyes, his gaping lips and parted teeth, his flaring nostrils.

Thumping, persistent heartbeats accompany the ominous, crackling orchestral score, which melts into a synthetic, atonal composition of long, drawn-out electronic notes girded by distorted strings.

In his flight down the path—intercut with those fear-soaked reaction close-ups—the eagle-eyed viewer may spot a single frame or two of the purple-robed figure, arms spread to receive him, pale face alight with hunger, a white imprint of ravenous anticipation overlaid on the darkness of the forest.

A thick root—drawn up out of the earth by some dark sorcery—catches his boot and he tumbles forward, landing hard and sending his cane and top hat rolling into the dirt.

The gentleman, feeling less and less the confidence bestowed upon him by whatever paltry station he fancies himself entitled to, groans in pain and frustration as he begins to pull himself up to his knees, his gloves and pants scuffed and covered in a thin film of mud. A small sliver of blood stretches out along his forehead and he reaches for it, finding a drop transferred to and standing out in stark relief from the fingers of his black glove.

Pale hands, with fingers unnaturally long and nails yellowed and razor sharp, snap out to arrest him by the neck.

A flurry of purple robe and stark white face and deep red lips and blood dripping from his forehead—and then teeth, terribly long canines emerging impossibly from a human mouth. Teeth, scraping against forehead, tongue against blood, then against neck and finding purchase in the willing flesh waiting there.

The gore in this scene is surprisingly explicit and expertly executed for a local televised community theater production. Rubber flesh and a geyser of red follow the bite, and the attacker's performative reaction to the ensuing spurts of crimson can only be described as *sexual.* Perhaps this is an obvious gesture to the symbolic form and function of the cinematic vampire—especially those depicted in the continental erotic vampire movement of the 1970s.

The effect is unnerving and arousing all the same, as the

feminine lips and mouth probe and suck and consume in this gross affectation of sexualized violence.

Before you can interrogate these feelings too closely, however, the film cuts to the eyes of the gentleman in close-up, wide with terror but growing glassy and dull. They rotate up to reveal pure white before the lids fall closed and the music grows quiet and distant, the music giving way to the furious sucking and splattering of wet Foley effects and liquid spilling over an eager mouth.

INTERSTITIAL ONE

Darkness, accompanied by muffled, warped snippets of synthesizer church organ soundtrack, wet sound effects, small arms gunfire, and the distant boom of successive explosions are all soon cleared away by a smattering of telephone tone-dial notes struck in rapid, jarring succession.

Silence.

A basement—or prison—is revealed by a single bulb hanging on the ceiling as it flickers to life. The camera autocorrects for the sudden explosion of soft light, giving the audience a floor's eye-view of the dungeon's dark corner. Bare floors and concrete brick walls are smeared with smatterings of white paint and dripping brown stains.

There's a glitch in the footage: a sloppy cut or a warp, jumping ahead. A box appears on the floor, set upright. Wires hang suspended in the air to the sides. Copper, maybe. Then there is another blip appearing and disappearing quickly, its image implying a dark, human form, draped in a blanket or rags, arms outstretched and palms facing us, head covered by a burlap sack or bag.

The person—assuming it was a person—is gone again, as is the box, likewise the suspended wires.

The lightbulb dims and the room goes dark.

COMMERCIAL BREAK ONE

An artist's hand-drawn rendering of the Front Range of the Rockies appears, the angles exaggerated and the peaks covered in white. The blue, textured background implies the shadows, rocks, and crags of those ominous monoliths both familiar and captivating to anyone who has spent time in places like Fort Collins, Boulder, Denver, or Colorado Springs.

Over these impressions comes tumbling in a whirling, spinning logo, which snaps into position, superimposed in bright red lettering:

FRONT RANGE COMMUNITY THEATER
THANKS ITS GENEROUS SPONSORS

The card disappears. A glowing green, digital vector wireframe rendering appears below, fading in over the mountains, a phantasm emergence from distortion on an old-style computer monitor:

MALTHUS CORPORATION, INTERNATIONAL
ARTS AND SCIENCES PHILANTHROPIC TRUST

The words and mountains disintegrate into digital-green static.

Cut to a slow tracking shot over a smiling, white, upper-middle class family running over a verdant green field, kites in tow. Mom, dad, a little girl, and a little boy smile and laugh as the kites fly high. Soft, twee guitar and indistinct vocalizations imply a calming, peaceful tone as the female narrator's voice intones the commercial copy.

"At Malthus Weapons Labs, we believe in family."

White smiles in close-up.

"We believe in America. We hire more veterans than any other commercial military contractor."

A flash—and the father figure here is in uniform, standing in formation with his fellow "soldiers," his uniform empty of identifying rank, name tapes, or patches, clearly pulled off a costume rack without much thought. We return to the idyllic kite scene, the too-handsome man smiling with a row of perfect teeth that has clearly never been subject to the malicious whims of an Army dentist.

"At Malthus Weapons Labs, we take the best and brightest minds of this country, and direct that intellect toward the development and deployment of the most cutting-edge, lethal weapons platforms and munitions in all of human history."

A pristine lab, where dear old dad is bent over a microscope, his white coat as ill-fitting on the actor as his military uniform. A woman approaches as the shot reverses to a medium two-shot. She hands him a clipboard and smiles her shampoo commercial smile, beautiful and empty.

"At Malthus Weapons Labs, we also have a higher rate of women in positions of authority than any of our competitors. At Malthus, we believe that women should be at the forefront of weapons development and research, because *Girl Power* means *American Imperial Power*."

The supervisor turns to the camera to offer a confident nod.

"We know that the fight overseas is always supported by the fight at home."

Footage from a Boeing AH-64D Apache Longbow target acquisition camera appears. The image is black and white, like old horror movies, but what it shows us is far more terrifying than any painted monster. Bright, human-shaped heat signatures cross a street in some desert village on the other side of the world—in a different world entirely, for all the connection it might have to the family flying kites.

A sudden flash of light and flame erupts, engulfing these forms. When the smoke clears, the men are no more, save for one. His upper torso is all that remains after the violence.

He tries to pull himself forward a few desperate inches, guts and shredded flesh trailing behind him in the dirt, but he has nowhere to hide, and no help is coming. The spattering dust-ups of a salvo of 30mm rounds sees to that.

"That's why we're proud to support local cultural efforts," the narrator continues, her voice sweet and inviting. "Arts and entertainment and scientific solutions to the pressing psycho-spiritual rot that even now gnaws away at your conscience and provides the fuel for your sweat-soaked nightmares."

Cut to the 50-yard line of a football field under the Friday night lights, where girls in their mid-20s playacting as high schoolers in red, white, and blue cheerleading outfits tumble about in front of a massive American flag. Adoring, overweight adults on the sidelines go red-faced with rapture and smash their flabby hands together in pagan worship. The football players—tall, handsome, free of acne, right out of central casting, in contrast to the revolting authenticity of the fans—hold their hands to their hearts and tastefully allow their eyes to water.

They all stand—all of those *ungrateful motherfuckers better stand, goddammit*—for the national anthem.

"Our grant programs also sponsor important research that is making a difference in the lives of young war veterans, those brave volunteers undergoing clinical trials for advanced, experimental therapeutics."

Cut to a young man, a scar along his face and tears in his eyes—tears of a different sort—as he is held down to a lab chair by figures in stark-white hazmat suits.

Another approaches with a dribbling needle, the light catching the silver liquid bubbling out of the heavy gauge point. The subject's screams of terror are silenced by the music, which swells with the military pride of marching drums and somber horns. The needle slips into his arm and there is indeed blood, as it is not a clean insertion. His young face twists into rage—and ultimately, acceptance.

Soon he is smiling through the tears, and the techs in the hazmat suits turn to the camera and join him in a heart-warming, all-American *thumbs up*.

"A combination of engineered cultural diet and proper chemical hygiene can and will make a difference in the minds of our disgruntled veteran and civilian populations."

Back to the family, now sitting on a blanket, enjoying sandwiches and bottled water from a picnic basket. A small golden retriever puppy, cute and energetic, bounds into the foreground, eliciting laughter from the stock photo humans. Black Hawk helicopters cut across the perfect blue sky behind them, flying tight in attack formation.

"Enjoy this local cultural event, proudly sponsored by Malthus Weapons Labs. Because every American needs culture. Culture engineered by graduates of top-tier research institutions to provide maximum psychological conditioning impact and desired political and economic behavioral outcomes."

The family turns to the camera to smile and wave, their perfect faces and perfect white skin and perfect hair unmolested by white-hot phosphorous or flesh-rending shrapnel or birth defect-causing uranium shell casings that their company produces and our military expends on foreign soil for reasons no one really understands anymore.

Fade to black. A moment of silence and hissing static, and the next commercial begins.

Establishing shot: a grocery store set at the far side of a crumbling blacktop parking lot occupied by a smattering of rusted-out cars, weather-beaten RVs, and pickup trucks. The sign above the entrance sputters to life with a haphazard glow: **QUEEN SU ERS**, the light bulbs meant to illuminate the "P" shattered.

Haggard working-class customers coming off of brutal double shifts, socially isolated elderly on walkers, and obese shut-ins on scooters stumble or roll slowly toward the automatic doors that serve as the grocery store's hungry maw. Piles of orange pumpkins set before the doors are ruled over by twin scarecrows, kings of their own opposing hills of supple gourd flesh.

The low-quality image and warbling audio cannot be ascribed to the age of the broadcast or the degradation of the tape. Compared to the Malthus Weapons Lab advertisement, this is a shoddy, local production, and the off-timed editing and badly mixed audio narration that follows proves this.

"At Queen Supers, we know how important Halloween is to our customers."

The candy aisle is fully stocked. Reds and blues and greens and yellows—candy bars and bags of chocolate, gummies and hard candies and suckers, smiling vampires and Frankenstein's monsters and mummies. Cartoon leers from spooky ghosts and costume-wearing candy company mascots.

"We've got everything you need to have some *ghoulish* fun this Halloween season!"

A baker pulls pumpkin-shaped cookies from an industrial oven. Dissolve to a confectioner decorating the sugary jack-o'-lanterns with orange icing squeezed from a white tube.

"From holiday treats to delightful tricks."

An aisle of costumes—cheap-looking rubber monster faces and plastic superhero masks. Fairy dresses and astronaut suits. Space wizards and vampires. Witches' hats and brooms. Cartoon characters and friendly mutants. On the lower shelves sit row after row of empty plastic pumpkins and oversized skulls, soon to be clutched in the hands of eager children collecting treats about town. The right-to-left tracking shot is a little bumpy and very grainy, but not disruptive enough to totally hide the blackened, flesh-dripping hands emerging from the crevices of darkness behind the products on the shelves. Reaching, *grasping*.

"Don't forget drink mixers and party favors for the adults!"

Cut to row upon row of tonic and seltzer waters, of margarita mixes and vodka slushie packs. A down-the-aisle perspective shot reveals a shambling, inhuman figure approaching from the far side, fire-charred flesh sloughing off of its skull and its outstretched, clawed hands. A fast dissolve carries us away to the next shot.

A mom-on-the-go opens up a glass door and fog comes pouring out. She reaches inside for a jug of milk.

"Don't be *scared!* We still have the essentials. And respectfully keep many parts of our store Halloween-free for those who refuse to celebrate the holiday on religious and moral grounds."

The woman closes the door to the refrigerated section and pushes her cart on. As the door snaps shut, we see a reflection—what should be the reflection of the cameraman, but what is instead a tall, viscous shadow. Set within its pitch-black void of a face are stark-white teeth and glowing blue eyes that trail smoke of the same color.

The shot shudders and the audio track compresses into lapping waves of distortion. Intercutting the shot are images of skeletal hands, frantically clawing at the dirt, out and *up*, an army of skeletons emerging from the earth to claim the land of the living in the name of the dead.

Now there's an image from of a handheld camera, approaching a coffin lying deep within the darkness of a forgotten mausoleum. Candles burst to life, and the lid begins to slide back, back...

Another shot of the Queen Super's entrance, its sign alighted save for the darkened "P," set against grim mountains and a whirling, hostile cosmos of night sky.

"Come to Queen Supers. Be subsumed by the dark. *By death itself.*"

Tape distortion and static interference spread across the screen like an unchecked plague. The static forms a great, living swirl, then assumes the shape of a leering, laughing skull.

"Queen Supers. We live in Hell. And it's all your fault."

The skull opens its terrible mouth, and we are pulled into the buzzing, static-charged void within.

SCENE TWO: EXAMINATION OF THE DEAD

The establishing shot is of a traditional half-timbered house with a sharply sloped roof, the shape of which is echoed in the panels crisscrossing the face of its upper floor.

The footage is grainy, streaked with damage, missing frames, and discolored in jarring, fleeting moments. Such Alpine houses surely exist in the ski towns and tourist traps that litter Colorado's Front Range, but the quality and degradation of the footage implies that these images are not original to this production.

The bottom half of the house is built of stone, old and well-worn by weather and time. The street wraps around its side like a snake constricting its victim, winding past its many shuttered windows. Successive cross-dissolves reveal a low door on the house's southern elevation, wooden and ancient. The door is meant to be an old servants' entrance or a receiving bay for the wine cellar, a space which has been repurposed by its present owner for another use entirely.

The final dissolve reveals the interior of the cellar, stonework walls and floor illuminated by candles. The candles are set within brass sconces fashioned in the likenesses of gargoyles, twin arms bearing them like glowing fangs.

Glasswork, moldering tomes, scrolls, quill pens and spilled ink, surgical tools, and more accoutrements of alchemical science litter the tables and shelves revealed in brief montage. Fetal specimens of various species—including some approximating human form—float in brine within thick glass and are underlit by flickering flame. Their dead eyes stare forth in silent judgment.

At the center of this laboratory is Dr. Betruger, a tall, handsome man of middle age with a heavy brow and thick, silver-streaked black hair. He is dressed in a blood-spattered white lab coat, goggles a-la the cinema-inspired productions of *Frankenstein* covering his eyes. He is hard at work with a bone saw, working over the corpse of the gentleman we saw dispatched in the scene prior, played with all of the silent, dead and motionless enthusiasm the actor can offer.

The camera moves in to reveal a sawed-open ribcage, a surprisingly convincing practical effect applied to the actor.

Dr. Betruger sets the saw down on a nearby cart and begins to probe the corpse with a scalpel that glimmers silver in the dim set lighting, alternating between the exposed torso and torn throat.

The wind outside rattles the glass windows. Candle flames flicker.

"Puzzling," Betruger says, standing upright and placing his bloody-gloved hands on his hips. "What manner of beast killed you, old friend?"

As Betruger deposits the scalpel into a pan of oily water—complete with a close-up insert of blood droplets trailing down as the knife sinks—Howard and Ellen enter from the streetside cellar door.

"Evening there, doc!" Howard says, leading the way down the slim and uneven stairs. Howard is rail-thin, his black peacoat oversized and hanging off his frame like rags on bones. His face is angular and handsome, his black hair complimenting the dirt stains on his face. Ellen follows him in and secures the door behind them. She is young, short, and vibrant, her movements exaggerated with the panache of an over-eager theater major drawn from the ranks of the local community college. Her brown hair is likewise matched by the streaks of coal or dirt on her face. Both carry shovels and lanterns, hinting at the nature of their occupation.

"We's just comin' back from making the rounds at the local churchyards, just as you told us," Howard says, helpfully. "All quiet on those fronts." His accent is a moderate cockney affectation in contrast to Betruger's slight Bavarian accent; his turns of phrase anachronistic, but somehow suitable for this faux-Gothic production of indeterminate place and time. "No disturbed earth, no missing bodies or graverobbin'... Although now's I fear young Ellen and I may be accused of such ghoulishness, equipped and skulking about as we were."

Howard and Ellen plop down on nearby chairs, setting their tools against the stone walls of the cellar and loosening their jackets and boots. They suddenly—and in sync—look straight ahead, faces somber, and make the sign of the cross.

"*God rest the souls of the dead,*" the both say. Betruger has yet to look up or acknowledge them, his eyes remaining affixed to the corpse of the gentleman.

"It was a precaution, a gesture at a guess, in the off chance that our humble burg might be suffering another infestation of Prussian resurrectionists," Betruger says. "I'm glad that is not, apparently, the case."

He pulls the bloody gloves from his hands and sets them on the cart next to his ghastly tools. He proceeds to wash his hands in a nearby basin of water, which is sculpted in the decorative likeness of a church's holy water font. "My autopsy is complete, although I have more questions now than before."

"Were you to saw any more, there would be naught left to intern," Ellen says, her accent approaching a French caricature, adding another ingredient to the vaguely European vibe of the setting.

"I had to check for evidence of infection or disease and, indeed, I found such signs," Betruger says. "A pallor of the liver and pancreas, a certain shriveling of the heart—all that beyond the normal degradation of alcoholic consumption and opium-damage to the lungs expected from the debauched lifestyle of one of our noble betters. That, combined with the necrotic flesh around the wound on the neck implies a vector of contagion that seems to have started and stopped, just as suddenly."

"Ghoulish business," Ellen says.

"Indeed." Betruger walks a few paces over to the wall, drawing a bottle from one of the crooked shelves. He takes a pull from the brown bottle. "I hope against *ghoulishness*."

"Mind if we get a nip, sir?" Howard asks. "It's thirsty work, all this patrolling against Prussian agents of forbidden science, dark magic, and the like."

"But you repeat yourself," Betruger says. He examines the bottle, considering whether to share such a spirit with his employees. Ultimately, he decides against it. "There's a bottle behind you, there. I don't share tumbler nor stem with the working class. Nor Catholics."

"But *you* repeat yourself, sir," Ellen says, finding another bottle on a shelf behind her seat. She pops the cork and holds the bottle high. "*Portuns un toast.*" She takes a hearty sip and passes the bottle to Howard, who takes two. After his pulls, he wipes his lips and hands the bottle back to his partner.

"I know we're just uneducated peasantry, born to short, meaningless lives of wasted potential and hard labor," Howard says, smacking his lips from the bite of the liquor, "but maybe we can help you think through your present troubles, sir. Couldn't hurt."

Betruger takes another swig from his own bottle as he returns to the body.

"Yes. Sure. What the hell." He gestures for the laborers to approach the corpse.

"From the beginning, then," he says, as if delivering a rote lecture at university. "Here in the burg, we have a series of deaths and disappearances stretching back at least a month, which, up until now, have been restricted to the population of the laboring, ethnic, and religious minority classes, and thus not worthy of official inquiry."

"If we were worthy of the Father's love, we would have been born into families of wealth and noble privilege, *oui*?" Ellen says, wide-eyed and blank-faced. Betruger offers her a warm, unironic smile.

"Someone has been brushing up on her Calvinism, I see. Well done."

"A priest, he taught me how to read," Ellen says. "The sheriff hanged him for it."

"Just yesterday, another body was discovered," Betruger continues. "That of a nobleman, this lesser *freiheir* of no little respect and wealth. Feigned ignorance on the part of the burgomaster is no longer tolerable. Investigation must be undertaken to root out this evil."

"I would hope and pray our kind master might pursue justice, should we go missing, or worse," Howard says, to no effect.

"The first assumption in any death featuring this type of disfigurement is wolf attack, or perhaps degenerate Hungarian highwaymen," Betruger says, gesturing to the wounds on the nobleman's neck. "But a strange infection within the body's systems gestures toward darker possibilities."

He drapes a white sheet over the body. Blood seeps through and stains the shroud.

"Cause of death is exsanguination. But all my years spent in the study of medicine and the phrenological sciences has not prepared me to face the dread possibilities that such changes in the victim's physiology presage."

"'Ex-sang...?'" Ellen says, working through the word.

"Somethin' et all his blood, love," Howard explains.

"Oh, of course," she says, nodding. "And his body—it shows change, like a sickness within?"

"*Oui*," Betruger says, indulging his foreign-born servant.

"Might it not be, then—the dread *vampyr*?"

Lighting crashes outside, drenching the cellar laboratory in a terrible white light. For one frame—and one frame only—a figure appears, arms outstretched, hooded head tilting to the side, copper wires extending from its fingers.

Synthesizer-organ notes crash. The lightning fades.

The figure is gone.

We are treated to a close-up of the basin of water, which reflects Howard's face as horror spreads across it like oil—or blood. He crosses himself reflexively.

"'Dread vampyr,' you say..." Betruger says, stroking his chin. He moves to a nearby shelf and pulls a dusty tome from his collection of medical and occult texts. Meanwhile, Ellen flings the top of the blood-soaked white sheet back from the corpse.

"Yes, master," she says. "Torn neck flesh and teeth marks? Could be that a ghoul et his blood from here." She points at the wound, allowing us another indulgent close-up of the excellent special makeup effect.

"It's just a—a superstition, m'lord," Howard says, suddenly nervous. He gently moves Ellen's arm out of the way as he re-covers the corpse. "You know how her lot are. What cannot be understood by drunken farmers and horsemen must be mysticism and the devil. Such tales are not useful for a learned man such as yourself."

"It is not a *tale*," Ellen insists, shooting daggers at Howard, who wilts under her glare.

"This book contains many—how shall I put this?— *alternative* theories of medicine and scientific inquiry," Betruger says, bringing the open tome to Ellen. "Is this the creature of which you speak?"

An overhead three-shot results, their heads bent low over the open pages of the book—the very same elaborate tome from the opening credits. Weathered pages depict detailed, intricately drawn illustrations of flayed bodies in vivisection, a ghoul leering over them: slouching and grey, blood a river of crimson dripping from its overlong teeth.

"'There are many varieties of undead, or revenants,'" Betruger says, reading from the text. The music is low and atonal now, underpinning his narration with a grave sense of unease. "'The most terrifying of which is the vampire, *vampyr*, or *nosferatu*, approaching a ghoul in countenance and behavior, but hungering solely for the blood of the living rather than the dead, particularly those of Christian faith and virginal disposition. Known to frequent graveyards and necropoles, venturing out from its coffin during the night, for sunlight is its doom.'"

Betruger snaps the book shut suddenly, causing Ellen and Howard to jump.

"This text is authored by a colleague, Professor Castleman, who works at the university. A mere day's journey away. I will send for him tomorrow—but I am afraid I must dispatch you two out once more. You must search the great necropolis of the Templars—the ruined fortress outside of the burg. If there is an infestation of these creatures, surely that will be their redoubt."

A wolf—or something in the form of a wolf—howls in the distance. Candlelight flickers.

"That old place, sir?" Howard asks. "What shall we search for within death's domain?"

"Signs of fresh blood and the bodies of the missing," Betruger says. "Disturbed coffins and sarcophagi. The displaced *dead*. If you find evidence of such things, flee immediately, but the more intelligence we have before Castleman arrives, the better. I recall him to be a ferocious, violent drunk, but he has since matured into a world-class master of occultism, second to none in Europe in the study of witchery and the blasphemous arts."

The wind or the wolf—or perhaps both—howls again, rattling the windows and making the house groan.

"Perhaps I will send you tomorrow. The night grows dark."

"We might appreciate the rest, sir," Ellen says.

"Very well," Betruger says, taking a seat near the cart full of bloody instruments. "Please, retrieve my ether. I grow tired." Ellen retrieves a blue bottle and old rag from a nearby shelf, bringing it to the good doctor.

Betruger opens the bottle and sets the rag to its lip, just as lightning strikes once more, and the frame fades to black.

SCENE THREE: THE TEMPLAR NECROPOLIS

full moon, grey and glowing against an early evening sky, dominates the frame, an apparition among the clouds.

A graveyard is revealed through a three-shot montage. The film quality, grain, and color correction of each shot is distinct, signaling their cropping from public domain horror films. Grave markers, overgrown and faded; crooked stone crosses and headstones; a row of family mausoleums in perspective and cast in a dull blue, shot day-for-night.

A dissolve reveals the graveyard's entrance: swinging metal gate doors of spike-tipped black iron set between crumbling stone columns. This is a bespoke set piece, lovingly crafted and artificially aged, set before a dark matte painting of rolling tendrils of fog, limitless rows of gravestones and the low, sloping hills upon which they rest.

Ellen and Howard enter from stage left, carrying lanterns and shovels. They approach and push through the metal gates, the creaking and groaning of hinges an appropriate accompaniment to the brooding synth-organ soundtrack.

In extreme long shot, we see them make their way across fields of stone, the light from their lanterns growing ever brighter as the world around them grows darker. They are superimposed over another elaborate matte painting that rivals the work found in any film of the Corman-Price cycle. But the shot is brief—brief enough that the impression of the landscape is made all the greater and more impressive in memory. To pause the tape and admire the work just might ruin the magic.

Ellen and Howard stand at the top of a stone staircase that descends into a limitless realm of shadow. The shot is set from within the crypt, at the base of the staircase. Their lanterns bob and flicker like will-o'-wisps.

The interior is lit by gradual, patient degrees of expanding light as Ellen and Howard begin their descent into the subterranean chamber.

"Why did we have to set out so late, when the sun is low and shadows emerge from their hiding places?" Ellen asks, leading the way down the stairs.

"The good doctor had tasks for me about the village, including securing a messenger for Professor Castleman at first light," Howard says. "And I'm still working off that ether hangover."

Ellen reaches the bottom of the stairs and holds her lantern aloft to light the scene—with some help from the cinematographer's soft lamps at the edge of the frame. The lantern chases the shadows away with each dramatic sweep of Ellen's arm.

"Here we are," she says. "These Templar catacombs stretch on for miles."

"And we're to look for signs of vile goblinry in this dark muck, eh?" Howard asks, with all the enthusiasm of a coward.

"If testimony of the devil's schemes is to be found, it shall be found here. According to the good doctor, anyways."

Howard looks back up the staircase, his face cast in pale blue planks of moonlight.

"The shadows grow long and my throat grows dry for want of the drink. On with it, then."

They move further into the crypt, swatting at thick spiderwebs and the dust specks that float in the air.

At the center of the set is their destination: a great

sarcophagus on an elevated stone platform.

Ellen steps up and holds her lamp aloft. Howard dutifully hangs back, his lantern lighting a row of coffins behind him and illuminating the crypt's painted set wall, complete with intricate stone bricks, alcoves, empty sconces, and a dirt-covered skull set within a square of black.

"The lid has been touched, its fasteners scattered about on the floor," Ellen says, inspecting the sarcophagus.

"Who would want to get into such a thing?" Howard asks. "Thief I've been, yay, I'll admit, but never would I consider stealing from the dead."

"It is them that might desire getting *out* that give me pause," Ellen says.

A chill wind blows through the crypt, crackling along the quiet audio track. They both shiver, and Howard looks back toward the staircase.

"Awful dark, awful early," he says in a stage whisper.

"Aye," Ellen says. "Let us be about it."

They set their shovels down, sending up little clouds of dust. Ellen places the lantern on the far side of the sarcophagus—for our benefit, no doubt—and Howard joins her up on the platform. The lid is slightly ajar, but only moves further with great, exaggerated effort from them both.

One last grunting, coordinated push dislodges the stone lid, and it grinds down to strike the floor with a sharp *clink*.

Ellen retrieves the lantern and creeps up to the edge of the open container, eyes just barely over the edges, peering into darkness.

"Empty!" she hisses. "I'll be damned—if not for the redeeming blood of Christ, the prayers of the saints, and the holy presence of His redeemed church on earth, of course." Ellen and Howard both cross themselves, eyes lifted to the cobwebs and crumbling stones of the ceiling above.

"Is an empty tomb evidence enough for the good doctor?" Howard asks.

"'Twas enough for Mary Magdalene," Ellen says. "This

is a crypt of the Templar officers, like to have jewels and baubles entombed which might attract thieves. A body absent its post, yes, but this does not prove goblinry."

"Perhaps it's resurrection men after all," Howard says. "Ill omen, this vacated grave. Let's have a further look down these underhalls and be on our way."

Ellen and Howard step down from the central sarcophagus and begin to investigate the rest of the crypt, their lanterns floating in the dark. Shadow and light joust along stone walls and their pale faces.

The shuffling of feet on cold tomb floor and the low moan of the wind outside are soon joined by another, more human wail, just barely audible.

Howard turns toward the camera in a close-up, the lantern casting uneven light on his worried face from below.

"What was that?"

"I heard naught but your stomach," Ellen says.

"Shh!"

A moment passes. We trade close-ups of the laborers, then coverage of the sarcophagus, nearby coffins, and a rat scurrying across old bones. The wind cries outside. Water drips on stone, somewhere distant.

Suddenly, the wail returns, almost inhuman—perhaps produced by a synthesizer—but surely no natural noise or trick of the wind.

"There, do you hear it?" Howard says, eyes sweeping the darkness in vain.

"I don't—"

The wail becomes a groan—then a growl—echoing off of the walls of the chamber, emanating from somewhere nearby.

"Time to fly, I think!" Ellen says. "If it is so important to the good doctor, he can come down here himself to—" Her words catch in her throat and become a gasp. Dread creeps along her face, sending her eyes wide as they fixate on the shambling form emerging from the dark, stage left.

Discordant synth-organ notes crash down as the ghoulish horror breaks from the shadows. Slowly, deliberately, its reaching arms dripping with grey flesh and rot-stained rags, its desiccated face emerges in the dull, flickering light of their lanterns. Dead-white eyes blink open and uneven, brown-stained teeth clatter between grey lips bulging with fetid gases.

The creature's head *must* be a prosthetic, a gag built in an inspired stage hand's garage, or perhaps the creation of a local effects professional, as the arrhythmic, robotic workings of its jaw and eyelids blinking over those dreadful eyes imply the cadence of animatronics, horrifying in their uncanny-valley unreality.

The gag's application to the actor is seamless, their true head and shoulders well-hidden within. The torso is rail-thin and collapsed, revealing broken ribs and the pulsing, wet heart of a corpse returned to life.

The ghoul's reveal is slow and its advance toward our actors equally so, capitalizing on the shock of its appearance and the professionalism of the special effect. When the camera finally breaks from the shambling horror, we see how terribly close it is to Ellen, frozen as she is in fear.

A pair of brief, clumsy reaction shots of Howard and Ellen precede its rotting hands finding purchase on the woman's neck. The staccato pacing of this sequence recalls real-life violence and the memories thereof: of how quickly events can spiral out of control; of how swift death might emerge from the corners of our neat lives to seize our souls in its icy grip.

Ellen chokes out an abortive scream and drops her lantern, which crashes to the cold ground, glass and fire exploding outwards—a nice insert pulled from another film with degraded and grainy stock. Flames spread along dry grass and old rags scattered about.

Howard, demonstrating courage we didn't know he possessed, rushes toward the ghoul, his own lantern raised.

Flames rise and dance before the action here, digitally inserted in the foreground of each shot.

"Release her, fiend!"

A close-up of Howard's boots reveals another pair of ghoul-hands emerging from the darkness, seizing his ankle. Howard shouts in surprise and stumbles, falling to the ground.

Ellen shakes off her attacker, shoving it back a few feet. The ghoul backpedals but keeps its balance as the camera moves in to its terrible, rotted face and snapping jaw for another gruesome close-up.

Ellen's hand finds her shovel, and in a cut-too-quick sequence, she pulls back, swings it forward, and sends the broad blade into the ghoul's neck. Its head pops off neatly and tumbles to the stone floor.

Howard, meanwhile, is being dragged into a wall of darkness behind a rotting wooden coffin prop, unable to free himself from the grip of the second ghoul.

The headless body of Ellen's attacker collapses as Howard's cries gain her attention. She moves to stand over him and lifts the shovel high, bringing the blade down on the right arm of the video nasty horror dragging him into the dark. Her aim is true and her effort is rewarded with a spray of garish, orange-red blood that erupts like a fountain.

Again and again she strikes, the blood a vivid arterial spray that soaks her face and arms and covers Howard in its wash as he scrambles away.

Interesting that the filmmakers would think the gore effects of this scene—from the preceding decapitation to the high volume of blood spraying all over the actors—would be appropriate for broadcast. It must have resulted in FCC complaints. It must have upset the program sponsors. It must have caused a reaction, one documented by government paperwork and local news stories or early social media buzz. It must have had *some* impression, left some trace, somewhere beyond the world of rumor and secondhand urban legend retellings. Surely your vague awareness of this broadcast and its legacy came from somewhere.

How else would you have heard of it? How else would the title scrawled on the VHS label have evoked a stirring of memory and excitement? Why else would you be watching *The Crypt of Blood*, if not because you chose to seek it out based on its reputation and legend, only to find it waiting for you in the hands of a man who wasn't a man at all? Why else would this all seem so familiar—so *inevitable*?

You sought out the tape. *You* have agency here. That's the only explanation that makes any sense.

Right?

Howard's on his feet now, armed with his own dirt-encrusted shovel, joining the bloody assault on the creature that nearly pulled him to his doom.

But a long shot of the set presents us with a new set of dangers. A second pair of ghouls has appeared near the stone stair, blocking the exit. They are cloak- and rag-wrapped undead, faces grey and half covered. Actors in makeup and simple costumes without more elaborate prostheses, yes, but the distance of the camera and the pacing of the editing gives you enough room to fill in the ghastly details with your imagination.

Ellen and Howard move to stand beside one another with shovels out like pikemen preparing to receive a charge.

"This is how it ends, then," Ellen says. "Murdered by devils beneath the earth. Better than starving for want of work and home, or being waylaid by villainous clerks."

"It's been a lousy life, but I'm not ready to give up the ghost!" Howard says. "Even the poor and destitute dream of a better tomorrow. Do not deny me that, oh Lord!"

"If die we must, we die on our feet!" Ellen shouts, swinging her shovel overhead and down across the shoulder of one of the lumbering corpses pressing toward them.

It receives the blow with a stagger, but takes another pair of uneven steps forward. The other ghoul grabs at Howard's shovel, trying to pull it away by the blade, black blood spilling out from its grasping palms along the metal edges.

Yet another of the undead rises in the foreground in a somewhat effective jumpscare—its torso out of focus as it obscures the right half of the screen. It turns and begins its slow journey to join the melee.

A brief montage sequence of close-ups follow: Ellen's courage, waning on her face; Howard's fear turning to madness as he struggles for control over his ad-hoc weapon; the grey-faced ghouls licking their lips or gnashing their teeth as they close in on their prey. The music crescendos, with thundering, doom-laden bass drums accompanying the high-pitched notes of the synthesizer. Death bears down on our heroes, as it bears down on us all.

Just as all hope is lost:

"Back to Hell with you, bastards of Satan!"

A new actor enters from the stair, leaping down with a dancer's grace, great, golden crucifix raised high. The camera zooms in on the religious icon, the bleeding face and side of Christ catching the pale moonlight and refracting it into a golden halo of holy power.

The grim undead recoil in horror, claws covering their rot-strewn faces in terror. Ellen and Howard capitalize on the distraction, planting their shovels in the guts and necks of the foul creatures who collapse beneath our line of sight. Foley sound effects—crunching cabbage, splattering tomatoes—give us all the impression we need of the violence they receive.

Overcranked, low-angle shots of Ellen and Howard striking their fallen enemies follow, as jets of streaming black blood spray up and fall back down to coat the lens of the camera.

The soundtrack grinds to a low, discordant halt, reverberating throughout the soundscape with the eerie portent of the door to your childhood bedroom closing, leaving you in perfect darkness.

A two-shot of Howard and Ellen, catching their breath, brings us back.

"Thank ye, kind sir," Howard says. "We were fit to be et by these goblins, save for your arrival."

Their rescuer stands up straight, pulling at his great black overcoat. He is a handsome, middle-aged man with combed-back silver hair and sharp features. Off the stair now, he is somewhat shorter than Howard and Ellen, but he carries in his stature and displeased-looking face the air of nobility and confidence.

"These are no mere goblins, my boy," he says. "They are the fruits of the working of the dread vampyr—lesser spawn called forth to wreak havoc upon the land."

"But who are you, and how did you know to find us?" Ellen asks.

The man grabs his black cape and whirls to face the camera in a flourish.

"I am Professor Castleman, pre-eminent occult scholar," he declares, "And these events confirm Dr. Betruger's worst suspicions. We must inform my friend, your employer, at once!"

The organ notes go high and shrill as there's a dissolve back to a wide exterior shot of the grave-covered necropolis, the flickering film image of the detailed matte painting all the more unnerving for its jittering unreality.

INTERSTITIAL TWO

Out of the murk of damaged and aged film, a yellow-ringed cigarette burn appears and disappears like a phantom crossing between doors in a narrow hallway. Floorboards creak as if some interloper lingers in one of the dark rooms of your home, unseen.

The footage skips and we are brought to a new scene—which isn't a *scene* at all—shot on a handheld digital camera, clumsily held and passing over familiar faces. This is someone's living room, with hardwood floors, bare walls, and large windows that open out onto a wide street illuminated by struggling streetlamps.

The young actress who plays Ellen is reclining in a large chair. She winks at the camera before taking a long chug out of her wine glass, the red vino sloshing about and dribbling a bit on her cheek. The man who plays Betruger is nursing a beer in the far corner of the room with a woman we haven't seen on-camera before. Howard's actor is here as well, clearing empty cups and beer bottles from the coffee table to make room for a strange, flat board.

Others we don't recognize—more cast and crew, perhaps—enjoy drinks and cigarettes whose curling smoke give the room a film-grain quality. A man and a woman drinking dark bottles of craft beer are still wearing the bloodied rags of the Templar undead of the scene prior.

The main ghoul's head—that elaborate, animatronic prop—has a seat of honor at the end of the table opposite Howard and his board, leaning against a velvet-colored, high-backed bergère, in the lap of a young woman idly pulling from a hand-rolled joint.

There is an audio track present, but it's distant and indistinct. It's a miasma of murmured words, creaking floorboards, and clinking glasses. A series of low, droning notes becomes louder and more persistent the longer these cut-together, handheld shots interrupt the film. There are cuts here, implying someone took the time to edit this sequence together.

The camera moves around the room, held by different people at different times to capture different angles. Eventually it finds its way down to the surface of the coffee table, facing Howard as he finishes setting up that strange, flat board and heart-shaped planchette.

Howard—or rather, the actor who plays Howard, how easily these things are confused—sits down, fingers pressed around a joint of his own. Smoke flows out of his nostrils and his eyes go teary, and he hands the cannabis off to a pair of rag-wrapped hands that float in and out over the top of the frame.

The bottom half of the camera's view is dominated by the spirit board, a plank of darkened wood and elaborate script, its planchette hand-carved and full of dark swirls along its surface. We have a clear view of the alphabet, numbers, and YES / NO. It is presumably an antique, but its surface is free of scuff marks and scratches, and the black-painted characters are pristine. The lettering and numbering is the work of a master calligrapher, its serif flourishes the perfect accents to the broad, sure strokes of the characters.

Howard—let's just call him that—calls for quiet. The audio of the room is distant and muffled, so you can't hear exactly what he or anyone else says. His hands are on the planchette now, and his lips are moving. He's asking a question—and then responding to a jeer from the corner of the room before returning his attention to the board. Fellow cast and crew press in around him. Drinks and cigarettes and joints and nervous fingers and eyes glazed by drink and smoke.

Howard asks a question. It's clear he expects an answer.

A low, terrible droning commences. It's a shaking, persistent vibration coming up from the core of the earth, ascending through layers of stone and rock and dirt and cellar and floorboards.

The planchette moves. Slowly, at first, but then in fits and jumps, so erratic that Howard can't help but wonder if his own jitters are pushing it around the board. Gasps and laughter rise from the audience who are just drunk and high enough to be open to the possibilities that a spirit board might present.

Howard mouths something like *I'm not moving it, I swear* or some such. It's safe to assume that's what he's saying, and although we know that he's an actor, that his whole profession—or *passion*, if he doesn't quite make a living from his craft—is based around false emotion and false character, there is no deception in the pallor on his face and the dumbstruck hanging open of his quivering jaw. There is no lie in the mix of wonderment and terror of his wide-open eyes.

We can't know whether the crowd is amused or scared or taking this seriously at all. But we do know what word the floating slip of heart-shaped wood spells out. We know what the spirit board says, just before the tape distortion overtakes the image and the screen is plunged back into static and darkness:

E-M-E-R-G-E

SCENE FOUR: SACRED RITES

The music fades in, warbling and out of tune, then snaps back into sync with the establishing shots of swaying trees and countryside that are a mix of stock or public domain footage and pickup shots captured by the camera crew in the forests near the studio.

These images dissolve into an overhead formation of five torches, set roughly in a circle, or—to the eye of the astute viewer who seeks out and finds occult symbology in popular media—in the five points of a pentagram.

Two robed figures enter the formation. One holds a smaller, makeshift torch, while the other carries a great, leather-bound grimoire—the prop from the opening credit sequence and Betruger's lab, we can assume.

Reaching the center of the pentagram, one raises their torch high, while the other lets the grimoire's heavy covers fall open in their hands, revealing a blood-red tassel marking the pages flooded with a strange and ancient script.

In a nice bit of expectation subversion, the robed figure holding the grimoire is revealed to be Professor Castleman, not some evil occultist or vampire. The figure holding the torch is Dr. Betruger, the reveal of his stoic face an interplay of shadow and light.

Castleman begins a ritualistic intonation, his voice loud and reverberating with the cadence of an experienced and charismatic priest in a stone cathedral—an effect accomplished through ADR. His lips don't quite match his words, lending the proceedings a dreamlike quality.

"Tonight, we honor two who have faced true evil, and prevailed," Castleman says. "Tonight, we welcome into our fold two who have proven themselves enemies of the dark."

Dozens of voices, speaking in unison, offer their response from offscreen:

"Enemies of the dark, allies of light!"

The overhead shot of the torches again—Betruger and Castleman at its center, now joined in vigil by a dozen more in robes, emerging from the darkness and trees to stand in a circle around the flames.

"If the lodgemaster wills it, then I welcome these two into our secret brotherhood, where all peoples are united in the struggle against the evil forces of the occult, against the foreign provocateur, against the Devil himself," Betruger says.

"Welcome! Welcome!"

"Although you are of a foreign creed," Castleman says, "and you engage in rank Papism, we yet recognize that you are fellow travelers on the road of light. Step forward, young Ellen, young Howard, and join the Order of the Withered Hand. Enter our circle, and stand before those gathered to fight evil in all its many forms."

"Come and stand!"

With that, Castleman slams the grimoire shut, then raises it high, revealing the signet on its cover: a withered and ruined hand, pointing heavenward.

Ellen and Howard enter the circle, wearing the same style of robes as the members of the Order, but with hoods down so we can see their faces. They kneel before Castleman with the proficiency of good Catholics.

"Having faced the minions of Hell in personal combat and survived, do you now wish to join our holy and sacred order, that you may continue to fight?" Castleman intones.

"We do," they say in unison.

"Will you seek the truth in a world of lies, provide light in the dark places, and never yield to evil until your dying breath?"

"We do."

The following shot is set deep within the woods, providing the merest impression of distant figures standing amongst the flames. Twin veiny, blood-red eyes fade in over the scene, wide with anger and hunger.

"Then don your hoods and stand in the flickering light of these torches," Castleman says. "The night grows dark, but our eyes are guided by a light that never fades."

Ellen and Howard pull their hoods over their heads and stand, becoming one with the dozen or so gathered around the sputtering flames.

"We hereby recognize you as brother and sister, members of the Order of the Withered Hand, esteemed elect in the war against evil, keepers of the flame in the dark, mortal enemies of Satan and his works, wielders of the occult forces of light, good, and holiness. Servants of God. Amen."

Castleman lowers the grimoire and nods at the two initiates. They turn to face the rest of the group, which has gathered around the perimeter of the torches. Light applause and smiles break out as they step forward to embrace their new brethren.

A dread howling fills the forest, echoing from tree to tree, shadow to shadow.

A two-shot close-up of Castleman and Betruger reveal their faces to be resolute and their eyes searching, staring off into the darkness.

Another howl joins the first. And another.

The howls become low and hoarse, produced by throats and mouths from things greater than animals—but less than men.

"Dread omens on a night of initiation," Betruger says.

"These are no mere omens," Castleman says. He looks

to the others standing beyond the threshold of fire. "All of you, inside the perimeter of light! I know not what stalks this dark wood, but we are stronger together."

Just as the first robed apprentice is about to pass over the threshold of the pentagram formation, a pair of stark-white hands emerge from the dark to wrap around his throat.

He opens his mouth to release a scream, but only manages a sickly gurgling as he is pulled closer to his attacker—which the camera reveals to be the murdered nobleman last seen on Dr. Betruger's operating table, *now restored to hideous undeath!*

His pale, blood-drained face dominates the screen as he gnashes his teeth—two of which have grown to monstrous proportions. An extreme close-up of his eyes reveals blood-red lines extending to and from the enlarged red pupils.

The nobleman-turned-vampire tears his hand away from the throat of his victim, sending blood spattering across the camera lens. He then pulls the apprentice close to bury his fangs in the wound, drinking deeply.

Ellen and Howard rush forward and pull the vampire across the threshold of the flickering pentagram. Smoke begins to pour from under the creature's coat and the flesh of his face bubbles and pops in sudden spasms of heat. His cry of pain is a shocking, overwhelming howl not unlike those that heralded his entrance, and he releases his victim to fall lifelessly to the consecrated earth.

Reaction shots of the members of the order and our principal players allow for the replacement of the gentleman-vampire actor with an elaborate, terrifying puppet: great smoke-stained arms terminating in claws that flail wildly; burning, pustule-laden skin; an elongated neck; and a hideous gargoyle's head home to long, pointed ears, great inhuman eyes, and jaws snapping open and shut by unseen mechanisms.

Just as the shock of the horrific puppet is about to be transmuted from horror to comedy, one of those wild claws strikes out at Dr. Betruger. His eyebrow-raised closeup is the last shot of the actor as a living character, as the claws slice through his neck flesh and trigger an orange-red arterial spray. Betruger's head tumbles—squirting blood from its severed neck—to the dirt below, and provides us with an end-over-end POV shot that gives us another fleeting look at that impressive special effect work before fading to black.

Castleman lurches forward to bury a stake in the back of the vampire-horror. It falls forward, hissing steam and gurgling arcs of black blood to signal its true death. Missing shots and damaged tape herald a jarring transition of shaking frame and warped audio, but we see images of more fiends emerging from the dark, swaying zombie-like among the trees, the moon full and casting the terrain in a vibrant blue glow.

There's a shot of Howard and Ellen—inexplicably carrying swords now—keeping a pair of inhuman, oversized claws at the edge of the frame at bay; stock footage of animated bats whirling over a black forest; Betruger's lifeless face as a shadow passes overhead; Castleman leading a charge of acolytes toward a tall, monstrous, seven foot-tall creature wrapped in ancient, decaying bandages and lumbering toward them.

More distortion and warp. The effect ends as the audio track snaps back to normal speed, and we see Howard leaning against a tree, his robe torn and tattered along his chest, revealing a great, gaping wound dripping with blood. Castleman and Ellen stand to either side of him, shaking their heads in resignation. There is nothing to be done.

"Got me good, that mummy bastard did," Howard croaks, blood dribbling from between his lips. "Ellen, dear, a bit o' the late doctor's ether, if you don't mind."

"*Oui*, my friend," Ellen says, offering a rag and a bottle of sloshing liquid. With shaking hands Howard accepts both. After wetting the rag, he holds it to his face and inhales.

"Ahh. Be right as rain in no time."

"No," Castleman says. "You will not. You have been wounded by a servant of the darkness, a summoner of evil. A *lich*. You will transmogrify into a mindless, blood-hungry ghoul before the sun rises. There is nothing we can do, save end your suffering now, and deny Satan your body as a vessel to work his dark will."

"Aye," Howard says, taking another deep pull from the lip of the bottle. "I can feel the end of it all in my bones. Do what must be done, my friends."

Castleman turns to Ellen, placing a hand on her shoulder.

"I will do it if you are too distraught, my dear."

"No," she says. "Although Howard is a degenerate syphilitic, he has been my friend these many long years in this cursed, foreign land of paganism and bigotry. I will do it myself."

Howard nods, a smile attempting to creep along his face, and failing.

"Thank ye, sweet Ellen," he says. "I pray that one day our spirits will—"

Ellen shouts and drives a stake through his chest, then produces a hammer to nail it home. Howard releases his death rattle, and the life drains out of his eyes by the second strike.

Ellen stands up, wiping at the tears streaking down her cheeks, but ends up smearing a stretch of Howard's blood across her chin.

A close-up of Howard's lifeless face accompanies a swelling of sad orchestral soundtrack. Blood dribbles from his mouth as he slouches toward the camera, eyes unfocused and unblinking.

The actor does a remarkable job of holding his breath.

COMMERCIAL BREAK TWO

oupes and hatchbacks, family vans and used luxury models, two-door pickup trucks, a small collection of RVs—prices *slashed!*

Gotta go, gotta go! All gotta go. We all gotta go. Run, run as fast as you can, away from the cold embrace of death. Drive a brand-new name-brand pickup truck over a mountain trail before the heat death of the universe. Before the cancer diagnosis. Before consequence-free police violence resulting in permanent eye injuries. Before we drop another bomb on a family of four in a country you can't find on a map.

Endless seas of blacktop, shimmering with heat, suffocating the earth beneath, fouling the air above. Rows of used cars and trucks. RVs on the back lot, visible from the highway overpass churning with pollution and human suffering. Lifetime warranties. *DEALS.* Prices slashed like veins. Brains dislodged by bullets fired from the family gun. Suicide-mess on the bathroom's tile floor, discovered by the children. Free oil changes for five years on all purchases. The owner of the car dealership is a real asshole who put his son in charge of sales. Junior has multiple DUIs and a cocaine habit. He'll be dead at 46 of either a stroke or an on-highway car accident triggered by a mild heart attack resulting from early on-set hypertension. He will have harmed a lot of people before the end of his life. They'll bulldoze a county open space and put in a private driving range named in his honor. After all, an open space *costs money* and people would just ruin it and waste it, anyway. Why go to an open space when you could be working, *working,* **WORKING?**

Tire rotations and fluid top-offs *free* when you finance on the lot. Competitive interest rates. Trade-in value plus 5% when you bring the kids to see the clown show. Clown show in the part of your mind colonized by the forces responsible for your economic and political alienation, every Monday thru Friday, before the first beer of the weekday afternoon. Get an early start on the morning hangover. Expired-prescription pain pills will take care of things.

No-haggle guarantee. Salute the veterans with our "combat discount!" Hearty handshakes and a tall, aging, reactionary man in a cheap suit to harangue you about "what's really wrong with this country." The answer may surprise you!

Feeling uncomfortable in your own skin? Ha ha, aren't we all! Purchase a convertible at a 10% discount and get a $100 gift card for hamburgers and cigarettes. If our nation's insane highway system doesn't kill you, the toxic food certainly will!

Smiling families in used cars, driving off the lot, entering a traffic snarl that extends into the pulsing, blood-soaked heart of a city whose better days are in the past, and that past is a lie.

Screaming jets overhead. *Salute to the Heroes* flyovers of neighborhoods riddled with gun violence and malnutrition and police harassment and novel viruses.

The police would like to have a word with *you.*

Your neighbors have accused you of being a degenerate loser, of being no use to anyone in a civilized, polite society. *Why aren't you more successful?* is the unspoken question hanging over the dead airspace of every conversation with your father. Have you considered learning how to code?

Your boss can take away your health insurance on a

whim, because in this country, you are *free*. Our forefathers fought a revolution for slave masters who looked west and saw the future, and that future was *blood-soaked*, baby! The ghosts of an entire civilization haunt the mountains, plains, forests, cities, and suburbs. Every square inch of America is haunted by the victims of genocide and empire, indigenous and immigrant alike. It damn well better be, or we owe horror movies an apology.

Stand up straight! You're a citizen of America, the laughingstock of a world we previously ruled and terrorized with bombs paid for by your tax dollars.

No 👏 *one* 👏 *is* 👏 *coming* 👏 *to* 👏 *help* 👏 *you* 👏.

How can an economically insecure patriot like you afford to pass up these great deals on low-mileage, used sport utility vehicles? Do you know how much human and environmental misery is tied up in the production of these babies? You want all that to go to *waste*?

We're proud sponsors of The Front Range Community Theater. This commercial is broadcast in exchange for a low four-figure donation, which we will use as a tax write-off. The dealership's owner will get to sit on the community theater's board of advisers, a position he will use to harass the staff and micromanage their day-to-day work when the mood strikes him. Better hope the troupe doesn't pick a play with any contemporary relevance on social and economic issues because, boy-howdy, that shit ain't going anywhere *near* the stage while he's in charge! No sir!

The shadow half-glimpsed in the alleyway on your way home from work is the vampire that will drain you of your life, one sucking mouthful of blood at a time. In the fleeting moments before your death, you'll sincerely thank God for not sparing your life. You'll think, *now I don't have to worry about my bills, my unfulfilled desires, and my sense of complete powerlessness in the face of systematic evil any more. Thank* God.

No one will remember you after you're dead. What good

did you ever do, anyway? What sane god could look upon the works of your life and pronounce them *good* on the balance?

Heaven? You'll be lucky to get Nothing.

If all time is simultaneous, the sun is already a dead star. All of human history is a tomb, a crypt of blood and suffering and dead time.

Free Carfax *(Abbey)* history report with every purchase.

INTERSTITIAL THREE

The lightbulb sputters back to life, revealing the damp concrete room once more.

The box appears on the blackened floor. A simple trick of editing, but startling all the same.

The prisoner fades in to stand atop it, arms spread, head tilted at an angle, mimicking prayerful supplication. Rags on his body and a bag over his head. A crucified saint in fleshly, statuary repose. He suffers the weight of your sins, in some abstract way. The metaphysics of the process escape you, but there's a certainty there, all the same.

Static crawls in along the frame, a progressive incursion. Waves of ants covering the corpse of a decapitated cow in the field of a UFO-haunted ranch. The audio track is warped and whistling and there are voices speaking in the practiced, accent-normative cadence of national news anchors. There's applause and faint images appear in the static of military men pointing to maps and charts and compliant, east coast media-types nodding and smiling before them like hounds waiting for scraps at the master's table. Such a simile is unfair to the dogs, to be honest. There's a nobility, a loyalty, an earnestness within dogs that these men and women utterly lack, and could never understand.

The static spreads across the screen until the bag-headed prisoner and the basement are gone, and within that wash of errant signal and dead air are the eyes of the dead themselves, shuttered now in this world, but open and accusing in the next.

SCENE FIVE: JOURNEY TO DEMON CASTLE ORLOCK

A still-frame image of the tableau from the opening montage appears, complete with open coffins and candles pouring wriggling lines of smoke. Text in an elaborate, hand-drawn script fades in over the image, blurry in its ghostly, lettered contours:

THE CRYPT OF BLOOD
SCENE FIVE: "JOURNEY TO DEMON CASTLE ORLOCK"
↶ TAPE MISSING ↷

The audio track is silent save for a hiss, an artifact of the transfer process, this being a copy of a copy of a copy. Corruption and bad data accumulate over time in everything, including and especially us.

The image fades to black, and in that darkness we stay a while. You might expect music, or a cut, or another sponsor break. But eventually, after long, tedious minutes, the hissing on the audio track is joined by the stilted breathing and mournful crying of a man. A man alone, a man broken, crying, crying by himself, semi-verbal gasps and wails escaping his lips, words spoken in a language you probably don't understand. Shuddering cries echo off of stone or concrete walls. He gasps for air and wordlessly begs for some mercy he will never receive in this life.

SCENE SIX: IN THE LAIR OF THE COUNTESS OF BLOOD

The film jarringly cuts to a close-up of a beautiful woman with pale, smooth skin, great black eyebrows exaggerated over her wild, blue eyes ringed by eye shadow, and her red, curly hair pulled up and held in place by a brooch; a great blood-red jewel like some terrible, dead third eye. Her white dress is all frills and lace and a great white cape extending down from her shoulders. The dress is marred by a line of fresh blood streaking down from her right shoulder across her torso—a crimson sash that accentuates her dreadful beauty.

"You are fools for assaulting my stronghold as night seizes the land!" she proclaims. Her delivery is bombastic and theatrical, long-nailed fingers pointed toward a stained glass window set within a stone wall at the center of the stage. Pictured within its jigsaw pattern is Michael the Archangel driving a spear into a leering devil underfoot, while above them both the risen Christ rises further into the blue, purple, and green clouds of Heaven. "No mortals who enter my castle shall live to see day again!"

The actress has obviously been watching her classic horror movies, as she throws her head back in furious, mad laughter that would make Barbaras Crampton and

Steele proud. Stage lightning crashes and thunder rumbles throughout the set; the faint light coming through the stained glass window grows dark and red, casting the players in cardinal hues. The patter of rain is a staccato soundtrack, underpinning the haunting, synth-organ composition.

Ellen, Professor Castleman, and two nameless acolytes from the Order of the Withered Hand stand opposite the countess from her perch on a stone platform where her open coffin lies.

"Your true death comes now, Countess Orlock!" Castleman intones, with all the gravitas he can borrow from Peter Cushing. "We reject your dark gift and all powers of evil!" He draws a longsword as Ellen raises a burning torch and the others reveal long wooden stakes from within the folds of their robes. Castleman raises a large crucifix icon. A stagehand above the set points a gold-filtered light directly onto the religious symbol. It erupts in radiant, holy illumination.

The countess curls her lip up, revealing a blood-stained fang. Anger drains from her face, and a satisfied smirk crosses her lips.

"You vermin upset the balance," she says, her voice soft, eyes wide and alluring. "I rule here, as evil rules everywhere. I offer you service as my familiars in exchange for your lives. Bring me fresh victims and offer your souls to Hell, and you may find in my undead heart forgiveness for your misguided interference in the natural order of the world."

Countess Orlock extends her left arm in an inviting gesture, and her eyes sparkle with foul energy. A synth-theremin motif plays just as one of the acolytes—hood drawn over his face so we can barely glimpse it is actually the same actor who played the gentleman-turned-vampire in the scenes prior—drops his stake and begins to stagger toward her.

"No, brother! Do not give in to her seduction!" Castleman shouts, holding out his sword to block the acolyte from proceeding. But the entranced man pushes the blade away and soon is at the feet of the countess. She kneels down, wrapping her hands around his shoulders and leaning in, as if to offer a kiss.

Lightning and thunder crash in succession, loud and terrifying, and the set goes dark.

When light returns—courtesy Ellen's re-lit torch—the acolyte is prone and bleeding on the stone floor, unmoving, with Countess Orlock floating suspended in the air above, her white dress now completely soaked through with blood, her face a nightmare mask of carnivorous triumph. You can spot the wires if you look carefully—but that would spoil fun.

"Fools! There is no forgiveness in mine heart! I shall consume your blood and swallow your very lives, and grow all the more powerful for it!" Her voice echoes and reverberates, many speaking as one. It is not clear whether the tape distortion creeping down along the right edge of the screen contributes to the audio effect, but it certainly makes the visuals more unreal and unnerving.

"Countess Orlock, ruler of the satanic castle," Castleman shouts, delivering what will be his final heroic lines, "prepare to drink from the well of your holy destruction!"

"Come to me, my children, and feel my embrace—the cold embrace of hungry death itself!"

A terrible wind howls. Ellen's torch falls dark once more. All is darkness, and the sound of scuffling feet and blood-choked gasps for air, of menacing growls, of maniacal, villainous laughter, of a sword clanging off of stone and ripping through fabric and flesh.

Flashes of lightning reveal the fight in still-image tableau: Castleman swinging his sword wildly upward at the countess, still suspended in the air; the other nameless acolyte, now headless and blood gushing out of his severed neck; Ellen grasping the crucifix to drive Orlock away from Castleman, now wounded at her feet. Through each glimpse of this carefully choreographed montage of a final confrontation, the organ has given way to a droning, discordant composition whose effect is chilling. Robed figures, not unlike those of the Order of the Withered Hand, slowly file onstage, standing in a rank in front of the great stained glass window depicting the triumph of the archangel.

Lightning flashes again, and we see Castleman thrusting his sword through the countess' back and Ellen burying a stake in the vampiress' heart. In that flash, we also see that the players dressed in Order garb have, somehow, changed costume, discarding their black robes for bags over their heads and rags draped over their scarred flesh. Many are missing limbs or suffering from extensive burns. The makeup effects are all the more terrible in the imagination of the viewer as the grain of the image and the briefness of the light hides any imperfections.

Ellen's stake connects with the countess just below her breast, the cracking of bone and the gurgling of blood thick on the soundtrack. All goes dark again.

The wind whispers its secrets. A wolf howls, sonorous and alone.

Candles alight, slowly illuminating the perimeter of the stage. First, a pair on each side, then a quartet in the back beneath the stained glass window. There, the extras once again wear their black Order robes rather than rags and burlap.

Small flames erupt on candles set near the coffin platform, allowing us to see Ellen and Castleman return the limp, blood-drenched form of the countess to her resting place. There is no music, but the wind and the wolf's howls have a subtle, rhythmic quality to them, an effect that creates a sense of deleterious despair.

Castleman, holding the countess by the shoulders while Ellen maneuvers her by the feet, guides the impaled vampire into her coffin. They release their grip and the body slumps into place. Ellen goes to retrieve the stake, but Castleman shakes his head, *no*. He produces a slim vial of water, holding it in the air upright, and begins to make the sign of the cross—a decidedly Catholic affectation that surprises Ellen, who echoes the gesture and bows her head in prayer.

Castleman removes the cork and is about to pour the water onto the still corpse of the countess when the candles blow out.

Distortion cracks down the screen like a bolt of lightning, and the audio track warps into a high-speed, high-pitched cacophony. When the tape recovers, we hear voices—some familiar, such as those belonging to the actors on stage—and many unfamiliar, those of the production crew.

"—lights back on."

"Camera two, down. No power."

"Where's the gaffer? Art, what the hell happened?"

"Nothing. We were preparing for the next sequence, just about to hit the—"

"I'm freezing in this coffin, John. This corn syrup is ice cold."

"You can have my cloak, my dear."

"A gentleman *and* an actor."

"I've got a light on my cell phone. Could I?"

"Just everybody on stage, stay where you are. We'll take it from the top of the previous shot. Mary, you have the shooting script?"

"Right here, John."

Small points of light appear in the static-ridden darkness. Cell phone screens and pocket flashlights, moving about the stage. Glimpses of faces—Professor Castleman, Ellen, the countess sitting upright in her coffin, and a production assistant moving across the stage, the light from her flip phone giving her the glowing countenance of a ghost doomed to stalk the halls of this forbidden castle forever.

Tape distortion invades the screen, scrambling the unfolding chaos. When the image returns to normal, time has advanced and the situation has escalated, as the voices have gone from annoyed to frightened.

"—belong here, we didn't ask for—"

"Don't touch me! Don't touch me!"

"Put out the candles!"

"—breathe, can't get a breath—"

The light from cell phone screens and flashlights are gone, replaced instead by what first appears to be more digital distortion—but slowly reveals itself to be flames. Fire, erupting from the candles, grown long and tall and fluttering like winged terrors of Hell.

The screaming starts in earnest.

The image and audio cut out for a moment, and we are returned to the concrete basement of the interstitials. The light bulb buzzes and flares. The floor is slick with a crawling, viscous liquid. Pipes groan and the walls settle and shift as storm winds swirl outside. Explosions thud in the distance. Fireworks, maybe. Or thunder.

Bombs.

The prisoner appears, arms extended, head sloped, gesturing toward something awful. Toward woe.

The basement, prison cell, or dungeon is there in one moment and gone the next, replaced by the stage's false crypt of blood, the simulacrum of the countess' vile lair, now reaching its apotheosis as a true abattoir of vile mayhem.

Flames lick at the fake walls. They consume the royal purple curtains set at the edges of the stage, which the pulled-back camera shot now reveals. They paw at the coffin prop and faux-stone platform. They dance along the flailing limbs of cast and crew alike.

An actor—Professor Castleman—turns briefly toward the camera, and we see on his burned and flame-scarred face not a look of pain or fear, but of joy. Of madness. Of wide-eyed, leering insanity.

Perhaps you can convince yourself that the image is too grainy, the shot too distant, the chaos of the scene too explosive. But in your heart, you know what you saw. Excitement. A thrill. A player undertaking his ultimate role.

Castleman—or, rather, the madness beneath the rapidly burning-off shell of the actor playing Castleman—grabs a piece of burning, damaged wood that came tumbling down from above. He swings his torch in wide, ferocious arcs as his fellow actors and crew scramble over and away from the burning set.

The Order extras, Countess Orlock, Ellen, Betruger, the gentleman, men and women holding folders and wearing headsets, a small group of young-faced college theater-type volunteers—why don't they flee, somewhere, anywhere, besides the stage? Why do they run back and forth and over one another, confined to the limits of the frame provided to us by a conveniently placed camera that captures this entire terrible, final act? Where are the exits, so clearly marked in public buildings? Where is the director or production manager to point them to safety? Where, as the flames consume the Crypt of Blood, are the fire suppression systems, the spray of water, the mana descending from Heaven? Why do dozens of actors and crew scramble and scream and burn alive and tear at one another here, in front of a single working camera, set to capture the cacophony erupting on stage for our benefit?

Then the profile shots begin. In all of these, the background set, just out of focus, is still clearly aflame. But these shots are of the cast, presumably in-character, eyes locked on the camera lens, on the audience watching at home, on you. The soundtrack of chaos and final madness recedes, and the synth-organ provides a slow, spooky sonata, comforting in its Halloween TV movie-of-the-week familiarity.

Roll call:

The gentleman, in one moment dashing and proud and human, twisted and horrific in the next, a combination of practical makeup and that gargoyle-faced puppet, man and special effect combined in a stomach-dropping superposition.

Betruger, the formerly decapitated doctor with his head restored. He tilts his face up to reveal the shoddy stitchwork along the middle of his neck. His face is a ghastly, pale green, and two small, barely perceptible bolts stick out of his temples. For just a moment—and perhaps it is a special effect or your imagination—they shoot off sparks.

Ellen and Howard, standing close in a two-shot, shovels over their shoulders. Howard still has a stake embedded in his chest, fake (?) blood dribbling out. Ellen's overcoat is smoldering and her face is slashed with blood—perhaps her own—and she smiles.

Professor Castleman, who had been presumably destined for the happy ending of sunrise just before the music swelled and the credits rolled, raises his hands slowly, revealing them as shredded, wounded, withered. The fingers are fused together, the palms collapsed, the bones malformed beneath twisted, ruined skin.

Finally, the countess herself. Pale skin and ruby red lips curled back in a seductive, come-hither smile. Her eyes are bright, too bright, and they appear in a slow dissolve across the length of the screen, her gaze drawing you toward her, toward the television set itself, toward un-death and madness that follow the kiss of the vampire.

One final burst of static and tape distortion. One for the road.

We now see the stage from overhead. The walls and props blackened and curling smoke, obscuring the limits of the stage and the limits of the frame, the line between real and unreal.

The world, and nothing.

The actors and crew are all there, having never found their way out of the crypt, out of the world they foolishly thought they could reproduce and control. They are just bodies now, corpses piled atop smoldering rubble, atop a façade of horror that is no façade at all. Burnt and twisted, heads caved by flaming debris, blood dripping from bite marks on necks. Limbs and heads and eyeballs and jawbones and fingers, scattered and bloodied and burned, together.

Atop that corpse-mound and among the flames and smoke, a figure stands. Bag covering its face, rags over its body. Barefoot, arms held out in a mockery of crucifixion, wires attached to its quivering fingers. Covered head bowed toward the wages of sin. Toward ruin. His, and our own. One and the same.

The synth-organ swells. The credits roll.

When the last of the film credits scroll up through the top edge of the frame, a new list of names begins. One that stretches on and on, back into the past and endlessly forward into the future. The names of countless victims, condemned to early and unjust death. The vast and insurmountable legion of corpses, interned within the true and terrible Crypt of Blood.

The credits never stop rolling. The tape never runs out.

JONATHAN RAAB is the author of numerous short stories and books including the forthcoming *The Secret Goatman Spookshow and Other Psychological Warfare Operations*, *Camp Ghoul Mountain Part VI: The Official Novelization*, and *The Hillbilly Moonshine Massacre*. He is the editor of several anthologies from Muzzleland Press, including *Behold the Undead of Dracula: Lurid Tales of Cinematic Gothic Horror* and *Terror in 16-bits*. He lives in Colorado with his wife Jess, their son, and a dog named Egon. You can find him on Twitter at @jonathanraab1.

Artist/musician **MAT FITZSIMMONS** has contributed graphics to the underground (music posters; surf, skate, snowboard art; punk 'zines; independent books) for over 25 years, along with fronting the savage rock juggernaut, Herbert/Automatic Animal (1993-2018). A life-long resident, Fitz lives in Santa Cruz, CA with wife Brandi & giant cat Chloe, where he draws inspiration from the shadows of the mountains to the depths of the sea. Contact: feralteethpress@gmail.com

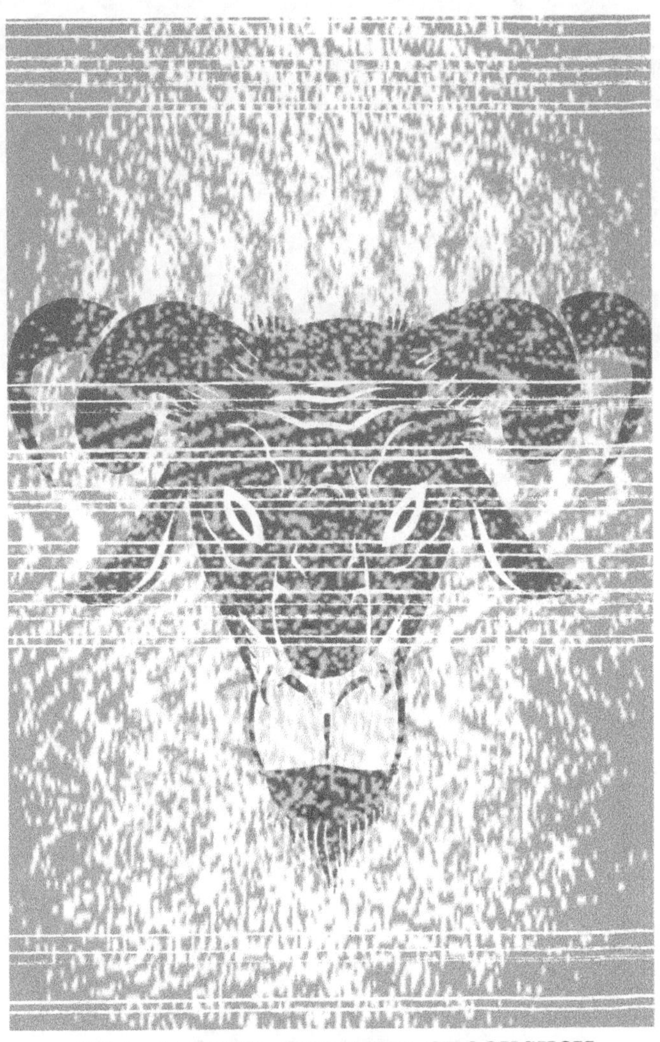

THE SECRET GOATMAN SPOOKSHOW
and Other Psychological Warfare Operations
Collected horror fiction by Jonathan Raab
Coming early 2021 from Turn to Ash